Never GIVE UP

Learning How to
TRY YOUR BEST

Jasmine Brooke

FOX EYE
PUBLISHING

Giraffe found it **HARD** to see things through. Especially if things were very **DIFFICULT**.

When things were **HARD**, Giraffe often **GAVE UP**. When she found something tricky, she often stopped **TRYING**.

But **GIVING UP** easily meant that sometimes Giraffe lost out.

At school, Mrs Tree told the class to TRY a new maths question. "It's a little more DIFFICULT than the lesson we did yesterday," she said. "TRY your hardest."

The sums were tricky but Monkey kept on TRYING. Bear worked carefully through the numbers and TRIED too.

But ... "This is far too hard for me," thought Giraffe, and she put down her pen.

When Mrs Tree marked the work, "Well done, Monkey," she said. She put a star on Monkey's book. She also gave Bear a big tick!

"Perhaps **TRY** a little **HARDER**, Giraffe," Mrs Tree told her kindly. "Don't **GIVE UP** so soon."

Giraffe looked at the star and the tick, and wished she hadn't **GIVEN UP**.

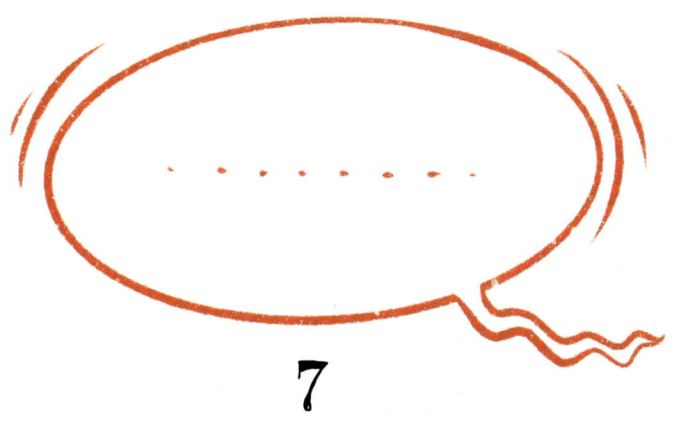

After break, Mrs Tree told everyone they were going to learn something new. "We'll **TRY** pottery," she smiled. "I want you all to have a go."

Zebra kept on **TRYING**. Gorilla had a go. Giraffe rolled her clay and tried to make a pot but it just collapsed – with a FLOP!

"This is too hard for me," thought Giraffe. She just **GAVE UP.**

Then, Mrs Tree looked at everyone's pots. "Well done, Zebra," she said, and gave her a star. She gave Gorilla a sticker, too.

"I think you should **TRY** a little **HARDER**, Giraffe," she told her kindly. "Try not to **GIVE UP** so soon."

Giraffe looked at the star and the sticker and wished she had not GIVEN UP.

In the afternoon, Mrs Tree said, "Let's play a tug-of-war. We will need two teams."

Wolf led a team. Panther led the other. They picked their teammates. "Giraffe doesn't **TRY**," thought Wolf. "Giraffe **GIVES UP**," Panther said. Soon, everyone had been chosen. Only Giraffe was left.

Mrs Tree had been watching. She could see Giraffe was upset. "Let's both join a team, and **TRY** our best," she said.

So Mrs Tree and Giraffe picked up the rope and pulled hard for their teams. This time, Giraffe **TRIED** very hard. She did not **GIVE UP**. Slowly, the rope inched back ...

and over the line. "We've won!" Wolf said to Giraffe, "because you **TRIED** your very best."

After the game, Mrs Tree said, "Everyone deserves a prize!"

Wolf's team won some cakes and Panther's team did, too. Then Mrs Tree said, "I have another special prize for someone who **TRIED** especially hard today."

As she gave Giraffe her prize, Mrs Tree gently said, "You have learnt to never **GIVE UP**, Giraffe, and that will always win the day."

Words and feelings

Giraffe did not always try in this story. She often gave up and that meant she lost out.

TRY

DIFFICULT

There are a lot of words to do with trying and finding things difficult in this book. Can you remember all of them?

HARD　　TRYING

GIVE UP

Let's talk about behaviour

This series helps children to understand and manage difficult emotions and behaviours. The animal characters in the series have been created to show human behaviour that is often seen in young children, and which they may find difficult to manage.

Never Give Up

The story in this book examines issues around giving up too easily and not applying effort. It looks at how not trying hard means that people do not achieve things they could achieve if they applied more effort, and are then disappointed.

The book is designed to show young children how they can manage their behaviour and learn the value of hard work.

How to use this book

You can read this book with one child or a group of children. The book can be used to begin a discussion around complex behaviour such as learning to apply effort and resilience.

The book is also a reading aid, with enlarged and repeated words to help children to develop their reading skills.

How to read the story

Before beginning the story, ensure that the children you are reading to are relaxed and focused.

Take time to look at the enlarged words and the illustrations, and discuss what this book might be about before reading the story.

New words can be tricky for young children to approach. Sounding them out first, slowly and repeatedly, can help children to learn the words and become familiar with them.

How to discuss the story

When you have finished reading the story, use these questions and discussion points to examine the theme of the story with children and explore the emotions and behaviours within it:

- What do you think the story was about? Have you been in a situation in which you easily gave up? What was that situation? For example, did you not try hard enough in a competition or in a lesson? Encourage the children to talk about their experiences.
- Talk about ways that people can learn to try hard. For example, think about how you will feel if you apply effort and then achieve something as a result. Talk to the children about what tools they think might work for them and why.
- Discuss what it is like to give up easily. Explain that because Giraffe gave up so easily she did not achieve anything and did not win any prizes. Not applying effort as part of a group also meant that Giraffe upset others.
- Talk about why it is important to try hard and not give up too easily. Explain that by applying effort and working hard you can achieve more and will be rewarded with the pleasure of achievement and other gains.

Titles in the series

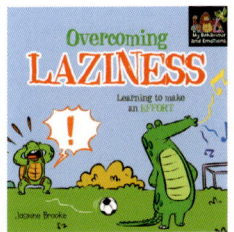 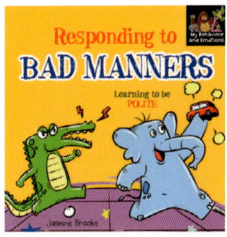 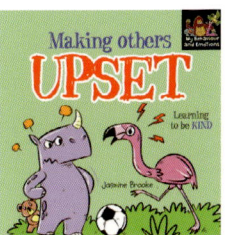 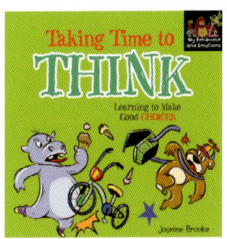 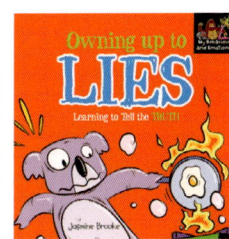

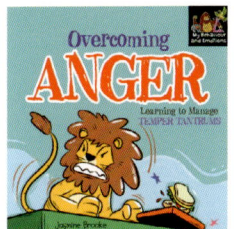 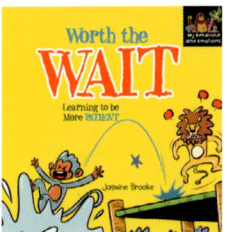 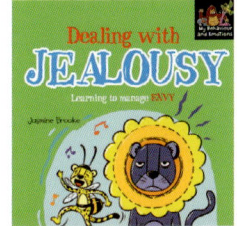  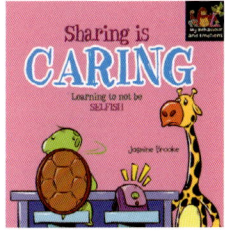

 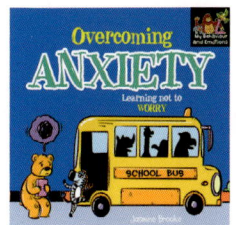 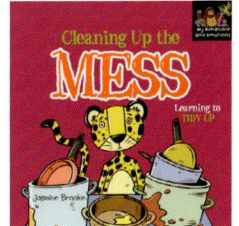 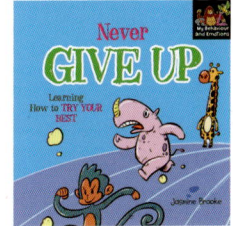 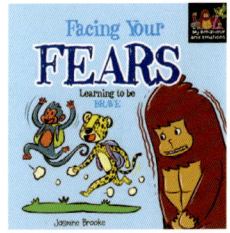

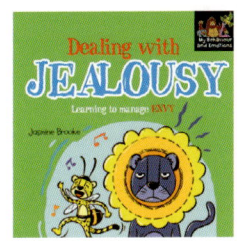   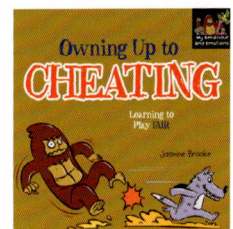 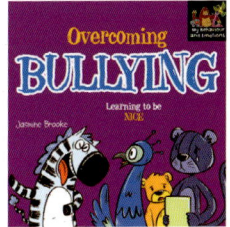

First published in 2023 by Fox Eye Publishing
Unit 31, Vulcan House Business Centre,
Vulcan Road, Leicester, LE5 3EF
www.foxeyepublishing.com

Copyright © 2023 Fox Eye Publishing
All rights reserved. No portion of this book may be reproduced in any form without permission from the publisher, except as permitted by U.K. copyright law.

Author: Jasmine Brooke
Art director: Paul Phillips
Cover designer: Emma Bailey & Salma Thadha
Editor: Jenny Rush

All illustrations by Novel

ISBN 978-1-80445-300-1

A catalogue record for this book is available from the British Library

Printed in China